Frequent Flyers

KC McCormick Çiftçi

One

T he first time she saw him, Hannah Carter could have been forgiven for missing him. The man had easily blended in with the sea of other businessmen on the New York to London red eye, and that's likely why her eyes skipped right over his tall frame, his relaxed, casual attire, the messenger bag slung over his shoulder.

It was only when he took the seat across from her, slipped a pair of wire-rimmed glasses on, and then dug in his bag to pull out a paperback that she directed her full attention his way, even going so far as to pause her podcast. A sighting of a man reading an actual paperback—and one that looked battered and well-loved, not like something he had just purchased at the Hudson News —never failed to get her attention.

If they had been on the subway, she might have assumed the book was a prop, some tactic he had read about—or to be more realistic, had seen on a video from some sort of bro-influencer. It would have been presented as some sort of novel hack for picking up women, similar to volunteering at an animal shelter just so a guy could walk dogs through Central Park and make himself seem approachable by the mere virtue of standing next to a golden retriever.

No, if this man had been on a subway she wouldn't have looked at him, his book, or his glasses twice, and she would have assumed that the lenses in those glasses were nothing but clear, prescription-free glass. Since she wasn't on a subway, though, she dropped her gaze a little lower, trained on the paperback that was now perched on his knees as he placed his glasses case back in his bag. She tried to see what the book was without staring at his lap long enough to attract his attention but soon gave up.

The cover of the book was face down and the spine was towards the man's navel, and it wasn't as if the book had fancy sprayed edges that she would have recognized from all the way across the aisle when he cracked its spine to begin reading. The book was so well worn and loved that its front cover nearly bent all the way around to kiss the back cover, again leaving her out of luck to spot any identifying characteristics. With a sigh, she directed her attention back to her phone, hitting the resume button on her podcast.

In her ears was the latest episode of one of her favorite shows, *Cases So Cold They're Frozen*, which was all about unresolved cases, which had become her favorite thing, unsolved mysteries. She resolved that the identity of the man's book would have to be just another answer she would never have, something to add to the list of cases the podcast had covered. Maybe she would have to suggest it to Zach and Tara, the hosts of *Cases So Cold*.

Hannah lost herself in the case of the accidental triplets, wondering right along with Zach and Tara if there would ever be closure for the families involved in that bizarre case of mistaken identities. She was hoping against any reasonable amount of hope she should have as an avid listener to the podcast, that this episode would end with no loose ends, every uncertain detail wrapped up with a neat little bow.

"Here's hoping we at least get a follow-up episode," she grumbled to herself as she stowed her earbuds back in her bag. The real benefit of listening to every episode of *Cases So Cold* was that on the rare occasion that an episode reached just the right ears, the one person out there who actually knew something about the case, and when that person called in...well the pay-off of listening to those particular episodes made all the rest of it worth it.

Looking up from her phone, Hannah found the man's gaze resting on her, a bemused expression on his face for just a moment before he gave her a small smile and returned to his book. She blinked, pursing her lips, wondering what strange thing she might have done to attract his attention.

Rather than risk making accidental eye contact with him again—it was inevitable, if she stayed in her seat, that her eyes would drift to him, work of art that he was, and that it would happen precisely as he glanced up, and that he would think, therefore, that she had been staring at him—Hannah got to her feet, slung her purse over her shoulder, and wheeled her carry-on away. It was always a good idea, after all, to stretch her legs just a bit more before getting on the flight.

Hannah made the trip to London so regularly these days that there was nothing about it that made her nervous anymore. A flight delay? That's why she always went on Friday, giving her a whole weekend to enjoy the city or at least have some built-in buffer time if the weather or airplane maintenance forced her departure time back. A phone running out of battery? Not that such a thing had ever happened, but even if it did, all of her arrangements were already made. Her reservation at the hotel had already been confirmed, and their shuttles to Heathrow ran at regular intervals. And what if she was unable to sleep on the flight? Well, that particular question was laugh-worthy. Hannah had approached every one of those early red eye flights armed with melatonin tablets, chugged chamomile tea on the way to the airport, and did everything short of getting a prescription for sleeping pills—the flight was short enough, after all, that landing before the pill had the full time necessary to run its course made her even more anxious than the idea of taking that pill in the first place. Of course, three months into her bi-weekly routine of flying to London to work with her colleagues on their various translation and publication rights contracts, she had never gotten more than a twenty-minute nap in the sky.

Given that sleep was her least likely activity for her time in the air, Hannah had prepared for every other possibility. If she felt nauseous or had a headache, she had a full first-aid kit of her preferred remedies. If she felt bored, there was always work to do or a book to read on her phone. And she had even once done something of an un-planned dopamine detox for an entire flight, on one of those early journeys where she hadn't made sure to pack her phone charger in an accessible spot. Rather than risking her battery dying, she had simply closed her eyes and entertained herself with her thoughts all the way until the plane touched down at Heathrow.

It wasn't her most preferred way to spend a seven-hour flight. There was a reason, after all, that she took great pains not to repeat it. But the way things stood, no matter what happened or didn't happen up in the air, she would be just fine.

Hannah ducked into the nearest bathroom, stopping to pee one last time before boarding since she never liked being caught up in the rush of airplane lavatory visitors that began their slow zombie march up the aisles as soon as the captain turned off the "fasten seatbelt" sign.

On her way back to the gate, Hannah briefly considered ducking into a newsagent, beckoned by the siren song of salty snacks and glossy magazines. "You already packed trail mix, filled up your water bottle, and you've got at least a few hours of reading time left on that thriller you got from the library. Just say no." She steered herself away and back towards the seat she had so recently vacated, her spirits dipping at the sight of the empty chair across from hers.

"Where did Handsome Guy go?" she mumbled to herself, darting her eyes around in search of him. When he was nowhere to be found, she sighed. "Not meant to be, I guess." She wouldn't have minded a chatty seat companion for the journey if it had been him. *Don't be ridiculous,* she chided herself. *Just because a guy is good looking and seems to have semi-decent vibes, that doesn't mean he can't have a mind numbingly boring interest in compost or the best system for filing financial records. Anything a regular guy can do, Handsome Guy can do, too.*

The next time she saw Handsome Guy, her stomach dropped with relief and something else at the sight of him. Glad to see that he wasn't just a figment of her imagination, the thought that the two of them might actually interact, that the possibilities her imagination had created could—*gasp*—become real, she sighed again as she saw him join the line waiting to board in Business Class.

"At least I know we won't be sitting together," she mumbled under her breath, that old resentment that Muldoon Publishing seemed allergic to prioritizing the comfort of their acquisitions associates rearing its head. She didn't expect that much, did she? It wasn't as if she wanted to be treated like a princess, to never have her feet touch the ground. But would it be so terrible to eat the *good* food on the plane? To use the *good* bathroom? To recline to a position she could actually sleep in?

That's ridiculous, she thought, getting to her feet again in anticipation of the boarding of the regular, non-business class passengers beginning. *I've never been one for a fancy feast—what am I, a cat? And their bathroom is probably the same as ours, apart from the fact that it's used by fewer people. The big problem, though, is the fact that getting used to that kind of luxury just might ruin me for the rest of my life. And that would be the real tragedy. How quickly could I go from being a regular, low maintenance kind of gal to being the sort of person who turns up her nose at convenience store snacks and the simple things in life?*

"Have a nice flight," said the smiling gate agent as she passed Hannah's boarding pass back to her.

"Thanks, you too," replied Hannah, before gritting her teeth. "I mean, if you're coming on this flight. If you aren't, then—"

"I know what you meant. You aren't the first person to wish me a nice flight. Not even the first person tonight." The woman's smile was warm and genuine. "I hope you get some rest on the plane. Enjoy London or wherever you're connecting to."

"Thank you," said Hannah. "You're really good at your job."

She chuckled to herself as she made her way down the jetway, shaking her head first at her own faux pas and then at the way a bit of genuine kindness from someone else could turn around what had every likelihood of becoming a shame spiral.

Nearing the door to the plane, she let herself briefly hope that she was about to walk through the business class cabin and that she might catch a glimpse of Handsome Guy again. She fluffed her hair, blinking her eyes open extra wide in hopes of erasing whatever sleep debt had accrued behind them in the last week.

Alas, as soon as she entered, showed her boarding pass, and was directed to the right, it was clear that the business class cabin was to the left. *It's better this way,* she reminded herself. *Walking through a business class cabin occasionally inspires inner monologues about class warfare and eating the rich. Jealousy doesn't look very cute on you, so it's unlikely you would have made a good impression on Handsome Guy, anyway.*

She made her way back to her window seat near the wing, settled in an as comfortably as she could, and took a deep breath. Soon—but not that soon, unfortunately—she would be back in London.

·❤·❤·❤·❤·❤·

Handsome Guy had become something of a fixture on Hannah's regular trips to London. They had never spoken, but at least every other flight they had a moment or two of awkward eye contact.

It was awkward in the sense that Hannah, at least, knew it wasn't the first time the two of them were locking eyes, but she had no way of knowing if Handsome Guy's eyes landed on her and transmitted the message to his brain time after time that he was making eye contact with a completely new human, a stranger who had never been seen before. A visual trigger that registered zero matches in the database of human faces stored in his mind.

On those occasions, Hannah offered him a small smile and a nod, a gesture that he sometimes returned and at other times seemed to ignore intentionally. When he looked away without so much as a hint of recognition, she was sure the heat radiating from her red cheeks must be making whoever was sitting within three seats of her think they were experiencing hot flashes.

But on the other occasions, the ones where he smiled back, she wanted to walk right up to him and strike up a conversation. Ask him what his deal was. Why, after all, was he so often taking the Friday night red eye from New York to London? Did he work in New York and live in London? Or was he like her, living in New York and traveling to London for work, but trying to make the most of it by giving himself an extra weekend to enjoy?

She didn't even know if he was American or British. She hadn't even heard him speak, couldn't even begin to imagine what sort of voice would come out of a man who looked like him.

Maybe the voice doesn't even match, she told herself, anything to shatter the illusion that had been plaguing her since she had first laid eyes on him three months before. *Maybe he's a voiceover artist, and he exclusively reads for chipmunks. He doesn't even have to put on a character, either. He just opens his mouth and pure chipmunk comes out.*

Whatever it took to talk herself out of a crush that made absolutely zero sense for her to nurture. She should be meeting men in New York or in London, but definitely not in the weird "in between" liminal space of airplanes or airports on either side of the journey.

Once again, Hannah chanced a quick glance to her left, to the far end of the row of seats waiting to board this week's flight. She chuckled softly to herself at the now-familiar sight of Handsome Guy there, once again reading a well-worn paperback.

She replaced her headphones and clicked the play button on her podcast. A day might come when she no longer had something resembling a crush on Handsome Guy, but today was not that day. It wasn't as if indulging in a little fantasy was hurting anyone.

•❤•❤•❤•❤•❤•

As the plane began to descend, Hannah leaned over to look out the window, something inside her loosening at the sight of this city that was like a second home to her.

London had snuck up on Hannah. She hadn't expected to love the city, and she had treated her first work trip there as more of an annoyance than an opportunity of any kind. By that time, she had lived in New York long enough not to get too starry-eyed about any other city. Sure, there might be some kind of mystique to a place like Paris or Rome, but a population center in an English-speaking country? Please. As if any of them could even compete in the same race as New York.

No, she was thrilled to live in the greatest city in the world, and her allegiance to her adopted home did indeed stretch far enough to make her resist experiencing anything new. She grumbled about domestic work trips—rightfully so, she was still convinced—and she brought that same energy when Muldoon Publishing informed her that she would need to make her first trip to London.

It hadn't helped that they had framed it as her "first of many" trips to the city. Without even having set foot there, she was already expected to make something of a second home there, with talk of her making the trip back and forth twice a month.

But when Hannah had arrived in London that first time, it was as if the scales had fallen from her eyes. She wouldn't admit it to any of her colleagues in the London office, but the mental picture she had built up of the city prior to visiting it was something out of at least the previous century. No doubt a side effect of watching too many period dramas, she had been baffled by the juxtaposition of modernity and tradition that the city offered. Sure, there were buildings far older than her country and those cute red phone booths she had seen on postcards. But there was also a young, stylish population, restaurants featuring cuisines from every corner of the globe and then some, and more opportunities to explore and discover than she had imagined. If New York had everything she needed in it, then London did too and even managed to condense it into a smaller package—and a package with a cute accent, at that.

It wasn't a chore anymore, taking these trips. Hannah even had a friendly enough relationship with Lane, one of her colleagues in the London office, that the two of them often met up on the weekend for brunch, a trip to the pub, or anything in between.

Hannah was already looking forward to her arrival in London. She pulled out her phone to check the forecast, smiling when she saw the weekend ahead was sunny with hardly a cloud in the sky. She opened her messages and sent off a quick text to Lane.

"Just about to take off. Fingers crossed everything is going to be on time, and then I'll have two full weekend days to be out and about! Any chance you're free to meet up tomorrow or Sunday?"

She studied the screen of her phone a moment longer, giving Lane a chance to read and respond to her message before switching it to airplane mode for the duration of the flight.

Sure enough, just a few seconds later, the typing dots appeared next to Lane's name, and her reply came through shortly after that.

"Always have time for you, love! Text me when you've landed, or better yet, when you've settled into your room and dropped off your bags. I'm free all day, and if you fancy joining me, I'm meeting up with some friends in the evening."

Hannah grimaced as her fingers began to fly over the screen.

"Sounds great. No guarantees about the evening meetup, since I'll be running on zero hours of sleep by then. I will, though, definitely be texting you soon. Have a great evening, and I'll see you tomorrow!"

"Can't wait!"

Two

Several hours later, Hannah was rubbing her eyes at baggage claim in Heathrow Airport. While she normally opted to travel with her carry-on only, on this particular trip her boss had asked her to bring along a set of thick, heavy training references on the art of contract negotiation for the London office. Hannah had insisted that all of these things could surely be printed and bound in-country for less than the cost of a checked bag, and yet Mr. Muldoon had insisted that he preferred to do it this way.

As the hard-body suitcase came around the carousel, she groaned in anticipation. Judging by the fact that there was at least a ream of paper inside the luggage and the unfortunate position of it—two bags had been launched onto the conveyor belt at the same time, and hers was stacked directly on top of a large duffel bag—she was probably going to hurt herself trying to retrieve it.

"Excuse me," she said to the people waiting between herself and the conveyor belt, jostling forward to get a better angle for her impossible task.

The bag came closer, and Hannah took a deep breath. Reaching forward, she wrapped her right hand around the handle, and she had almost managed to shift the suitcase off the duffel bag when the worst thing she could have imagined happened.

Straining to reach, she realized only too late that the firm object behind her left foot, the entire counterbalance that was keeping her upright as she balanced precariously and reached farther than her natural wingspan...well, at the precise moment that she slipped and fell, she realized that the solid object behind her foot was actually a luggage cart and it was decidedly *not* in the upright and locked position.

Hannah came crashing down onto the conveyor belt, her butt landing squarely on the duffel bag while her right hand never let go of her suitcase and her left hand clutched her carry-on to her side. She had spun around in the hustle and bustle of it all, finding herself sitting on the duffel bag, facing out to her gobsmacked fellow passengers, while she began to rotate around the luggage carousel at a pace much faster than it had appeared when she was on the other side of things.

A nervous laugh barked out of her lips before she could stop it. "Um...uh...what the hell?" she sputtered, trying to get to her feet and yet refusing to let go of her death grip on the suitcase.

"Allow me?" said a deep voice, and she looked ahead, tracking the direction the conveyor was taking her, to find a man—no, not any man, but *the* man—looking down at her with his hand outstretched. Just behind him, she could make out the mysterious hole in the wall through which the conveyor belt disappeared before reappearing a few yards down the wall.

Hannah tried to scramble to her feet, the very idea of what might await on the other side of that wall—or of what *trouble* she might get in for appearing back there where she definitely wasn't supposed to be—adding a healthy layer of panic to the sheer embarrassing cringe fest she was already experiencing.

"Alright, then," said the man, and then he was placing a hand on either side of her torso and bodily hauling her to her feet.

"I'm really sorry about this," he was saying, and the words and his English accent took a moment to become clear through the static that was broadcasting inside her skull. "It does feel quite caveman-like to be grabbing a lady without her consent, but you do seem to be in such a state of shock that it might have taken you a few more turns around the merry-go-round before you saw fit to exit the ride."

She was on her feet then, blinking up at him, taking a moment to regain her bearings.

"I...uh." She cleared her throat. "Thank you. I totally froze." She looked down at her hand, surprised to find the massive suitcase was still firmly clutched in her grip.

She gasped. "You lifted me *and* this thing? You didn't hurt yourself, did you?"

The man shook his head. "The suitcase nearly took me out at the shins, but that was the extent of it. Of course, I *was* hoping just to extract you from the belt and then to help you with the luggage when it came around the next time, but...well, best laid plans and all that."

Hannah felt her cheeks heat. Of course she could have just released the bag, could have waited for it to come around. Maybe by the time she had seen it again, the offending duffel bag would have been extricated.

"I don't know why I reacted like that. Again, I'm so sorry."

He dismissed her concerns with a shake of his head. "Don't be. As you no doubt know, the stress response is aptly referred to as the fight-or-flight response. There is, however, another response that should be included in there, which is the freeze response. Of course, there's also the fawn response, but that's really a story for another day." He cleared his throat. "Anyway, I'd say in a situation like this, it is perfectly within the realm of normal responses to freeze. I'm just glad you didn't try to fight me off when I helped you."

"Thank you again for helping me," she said, unable to stop smiling at the way his overly detailed explanation had tumbled out of him. Whether he was just the type of guy to want to explain everything or he was actually trying to make her feel better and reassure her that she was only human, it had at least worked to take her mind off her embarrassment.

"Hold that thought," he said, holding up a finger before taking two long strides back to the conveyer belt and grabbing the duffel bag that she had been sitting on so recently. He held it aloft, something like victory on his face.

Hannah winced. "That was your bag?"

"Was and is," he replied, smiling at her.

"I hope there wasn't anything too precious in there. Nothing that couldn't handle the full weight of a grown woman plopped right on top of it."

His eyes widened. "I'm not even sure where to begin addressing those concerns. First, there's the fact that the force this bag likely encountered being tossed into and out of various compartments, colliding with other heavier pieces of luggage, has already thoroughly tested its durability. But there's also the fact that precious and breakable things...well, I wouldn't be likely to put them in my checked bag, now would I? Better to keep them in my carry-on where I and only I am responsible for their security. Of course, if there were some sort of necessity where I had to check something precious, I'd likely have made a better choice than this old thing." He held up the duffel, and Hannah saw for the first time just how worn and rugged it looked.

"Fair enough," she said, unable to stop herself from cocking her head slightly, her inner curious puppy emerging. *It would be rude to ask him why he talked so much, why he felt the need to explain himself so thoroughly to a complete stranger*, she reminded herself. And even with the lowered inhibitions that came along with the exhaustion of a red eye flight, she was still able to stop herself from asking.

Maybe he's an engineer, she thought. *One of those analytical and literal minds that doesn't leave room for artistic license or any sort of inaccuracy. Or maybe he's just as jet-lagged as I am. Or hell, maybe he* was *being funny, and I just can't appreciate it because British humor is still too dry for my taste.*

"Well anyway," she said, with one final nod, "thanks again. I really do appreciate it." She gave him a smile, turned, and made her way out to where she knew the hotel's shuttle would be waiting.

"Take care!" she heard him call when she was just a few steps away. "Enjoy your trip, and watch out for escalators, the gap on the Tube, and make sure to look both ways when you cross the street."

She shook her head as she chuckled softly. What an odd duck he was. It just went to show that you shouldn't judge a book by its cover. While Handsome Guy had earned his nickname with his appearance, after interacting with him, it was safe to say that was not his most distinguishing characteristic.

Two hours later, Hannah had showered, unpacked her suitcase, and was on her way to meet Lane for a late lunch. Lane had told her about a cute little curry spot within walking distance of the hotel, and Hannah was grateful for the opportunity to stretch her legs.

She stifled a yawn as she turned the last corner, her lips spreading into a broad smile at the sight of Lane's curls bouncing as her friend rocked up and down on her toes.

"Hannah! You're here!" cried Lane, pulling her into an embrace and nearly off her balance.

"Indeed, I am." Hannah released her friend and gave her a quizzical look. "Though I was also here pretty recently. Two weeks ago, if I'm not mistaken." She held up her hands. "Not that I'm not grateful for the warm reception. I'm just not sure I deserve it."

Lane slung her arm through Hannah's and steered her towards the restaurant. "Nonsense. It's always a delight to see you." She sighed. "But there may be another factor at play here."

"Oh?" Hannah raised an eyebrow.

Lane shrugged. "Stuart and I are finished. Could very much use a nice day out with a friend." She worked her elbow into Hannah's side with a little more force than necessary. "And if I can use that to guilt you into joining us for a night out this evening, then even better."

Hannah winced at that. "I'm so sorry, Lane. He seemed like a really nice guy, and you're definitely going to have to tell me all about it."

"Oh, that was already the plan."

The conversation paused for a moment as their server directed them to a table on the sidewalk in front of the restaurant, leaving them with their menus to peruse.

"It's probably going to be a bit of a wallow, to be honest," said Lane when she looked up from her menu. "I don't even care if it's technically too early to start drinking for the evening. There must be some kind of special exemption for cases of breakups." She narrowed her eyes at Hannah, who was still trailing her finger down the list of beverage options. "And don't think I'm going to let you off the hook tonight just because you're here with me now." She narrowed her eyes across the table. "I mean it. I'm serious."

Hannah reached over and took her friend's hand. "I'm here for you. Seriously. I will do the best I can, but you know how these things tend to go. By eight o'clock at night, I'm slurring my words like I'm a college student knee-deep in a keg, and that's on *maybe* half a glass of wine. Staying up all night just doesn't work the way it used to. Unlike that hypothetical college student, I'm not twenty-one anymore."

Lane gave her a close-lipped smile of sorts, her lips forming a straight line. "You're right. I'm being selfish, and I can't ask you to sacrifice your health for me just because I need a bit of girl talk."

"I never said you were selfish, and if the court reporter will read back the transcript of our conversation, you'll see that I'm telling the truth." She squeezed Lane's hand. "Tell me what happened. I need to know how much I'm supposed to hate Stuart." She had met Lane's ex a few times over the course of her London trips, and hating him was going to take some major mental gymnastics. Stuart had always been kind, and he and Lane had seemed like the perfect couple. If they couldn't be happy together, then it raised all sorts of questions about who could actually make it.

Lane groaned. "Don't hate him. *I* don't hate him, so I can't see how you could find a reason to if I can't."

"So what happened then?"

Lane pursed her lips. "Why don't we order first? When I start telling this story, only the most oblivious server in the country is going to want to interrupt us."

Hannah chuckled. "A good point, as always."

Once the two friends had placed their orders, Hannah leaned forward, just managing to stop herself from resting her elbows on the table.

"So?"

Lane shrugged. "So...yeah. It seems like it's over. Stuart told me a week ago that his company is relocating him outside of the city, that they need him in Cornwall to take on a managerial role in their office there. It's a promotion for him, so I'm tickled about that, but...well. He's moving."

Hannah winced. "And he didn't ask you to move with him?" She couldn't imagine how that must have stung.

"Well, no." Lane took a sip of her drink. "I guess technically he did ask me to go with him, but he did it in that sort of way where you know he really wants you to say no. You know what I mean?"

Hannah shook her head. "What did he say?"

"It was just this really waffley, 'I know you wouldn't want to come with me if I asked, and I don't want you to feel any pressure at all to come, so don't even worry about it.'"

"It doesn't sound like there was even a question in there."

"No. There wasn't."

"And you didn't want to correct him and tell him that of course you would want to go with him?" Hannah frowned. "Would you, though? I thought you loved living here."

"Of course I love London. But I love—or at least I *loved*...oh, who am I kidding. I *love* Stuart more. We could have made it work in Cornwall, or maybe we would have found our way back here at some point."

"I'm confused." Hannah gave her friend an apologetic smile. "It might be the jet lag talking, but I'm having a hard time understanding why this all led to a big breakup.

Surely, if you're willing to move and he's nice enough not to even try to pressure you to do something he thinks you don't want to do...well surely, then the two of you can make this work."

"It's the wrong energy, Hannah," said Lane, a no-nonsense look in her eyes. "I don't think he wants me there enough. And it makes me wonder if this all was just an excuse to leave me."

"I don't believe that."

"Well, you don't have to. But I do." She took another sip of her drink. "Tell me something to take my mind off things. It's no fun trying to wallow with someone who can't quite manage to find the way to seeing my side of things."

"I do see your side of things. I'm here for you." Hannah's smile was sad. "I think I'm just in the denial stage of grief. I really liked you and Stuart together."

"I did too," Lane admitted, her eyes filling with tears. "So, where's that distraction when I need it?"

"Oh, I know just the thing to take your mind off it. I fell onto the conveyor belt at baggage claim and was rescued by a handsome knight in shining armor."

Lane almost spit out her sip. "Oh, this will do nicely..."

Three

When the tears in Lane's eyes had finally spilled, the result of her laughter at Hannah's antics in the international baggage claim at Heathrow, she took a deep breath, leaned back in her chair, and wiped them away.

"Thank you for that," she said, looking lighter than she had since they had taken their seats. "I needed it. You're a good storyteller, too. I wish I'd been there to witness it myself, but I almost feel like I was, oddly enough."

"Then I'm glad I spared no expense at sharing all the embarrassing gory details with you," said Hannah, smiling back at her friend. "If you'd been there, I like to think you might have helped me and I could have been spared the whole cringeworthy interaction with Handsome Guy."

Lane looked impressed. "Well then. Your savior already has a nickname? I'd have guessed you would have chosen something more relevant to...oh, perhaps the fact that he saved you from the baggage claim. Surely that's a more distinguishing characteristic than his face? For how much you seemed to be in shock, I'm not entirely sure I'd trust your judgment of what his face even looked like."

"Ah, well." Hannah shrugged. "You got me there. The truth is, this wasn't the first time I've laid eyes on this man, and today definitely isn't the day that he earned his Handsome Guy nickname."

"Oh?" Lane took a bite of her curry, watching Hannah with expectation and wide eyes.

"He's on my flight to London quite frequently, actually," she said, playing at a nonchalance she didn't feel.

"Well, this just got interesting." Lane set down her fork on the table and leaned forward. "Tell me everything."

Two weeks later, Hannah was back at JFK. She made her way through the security line, grateful once again that Muldoon Publishing had treated her to a Fast Pass subscription. *If you're going to spend as much time in an airport as I do*, she told herself, *as little of it as possible should be spent in lines.*

Something inside her fluttered with anticipation at the thought that Handsome Guy might be on her flight. Despite the oddness and embarrassing nature of their first ever interaction, she couldn't help but hope that she might see him again.

Not that she knew how she would react if she *did* see him again. It was entirely possible that her cheeks would once again flare bright red, and she would duck down behind a row of chairs, drawing attention to herself while also hoping to be invisible.

She found her way to her gate. Thankfully, it did seem that her flight almost always left from the same gate, and there was something very comforting about gate B22. It was familiar, like a third home. At this point, she wasn't sure if her studio apartment or her hotel room in London was her first home, but this gate was definitely the third after those two.

As she approached the gate, she didn't see the familiar outline of Handsome Guy's profile, and she felt something loosen.

It was disappointment, but it was relief too. She didn't need to scramble to think of what to say next. She didn't need to worry about how he was perceiving her. She could just be.

She took a seat in a familiar bank of chairs, a spot that was far enough back not to be the first to fill with passengers, and yet where she had a good view of the gate and of the airline employees working there. She could anticipate when they were about to make an announcement with almost 100% accuracy.

She settled into that prime location, retrieved her ear buds, and was about to treat herself to the newest episode of *Cases So Cold* when she heard a throat clear over her shoulder.

She looked up and was shocked to see Handsome Guy was towering over her, looking like he was embarrassed.

That can't be right, she thought. *I'm the one who should be embarrassed.* But then, as she smiled up at him in question, she remembered the oddness of their prior interaction and let herself wonder for just a moment if he might be remembering the same.

Oh, it was clear to her that if there was anyone who should be cringing at their own behavior, anyone who should be embarrassed, it was her. If there was anyone whose behavior would have made great fodder for a viral short video, it was her. She had ridden his duffel bag almost into the wall, after all.

But she did have just enough awareness of human nature to wonder for a second if Handsome Guy's own behavior was causing him some kind of turmoil similar to hers. *Or maybe,* she thought, *someone* did *record a video of me in the baggage claim and it* has *gone viral and he's embarrassed on my behalf. Oh god, why didn't I even check? What would I have searched? Woman on baggage carousel at Heathrow? Yeah, that seems like exactly what I should have searched, and now I'm not sure why I didn't.*

By the time she had reached that conclusion, it seemed an awkward enough amount of time had passed, so she spoke.

"Hi."

That was all she said. And she let out a sniff of laughter at her own eloquence.

"How's it going?" she asked.

"Very well, thank you," he said. He gestured to the open seat next to her. "Do you mind if I sit down there?"

" Of course!" she blurted. "I mean, of course not, go ahead."

"Thanks," he said, taking the seat next to hers and keeping his eyes on her the entire time. "Are you all right?" he asked. "No lingering effects from your mishap, I mean."

Hannah dropped her head back. "Oh, I was hoping we were going to pretend that didn't happen," she said, and then laughed. "But of course, we can't. That's probably the most interesting thing that's happened to either of us in a long time."

She returned her head to level and met his gaze. "But I'm fine. I wasn't even sore the next morning, so I suppose I owe you a debt of gratitude for the softness of your duffel bag. If it had been something else in there, I might have bruised my tailbone."

Handsome Guy shook his head. "That's the other thing, isn't it? When you walked away, I realized I had given you some kind of lecture about my own packing etiquette, I think? I'm not entirely sure what I said. The words just sort of came. But I am a bit concerned that I might not have made the best first impression."

Hannah had to laugh at that. "Oh sure, *you* might not have made the best first impression. I'm sorry. I was too busy turning the process of retrieving one's baggage into a carnival ride to worry much about anyone else's first impressions."

She tilted her head to the side, as if willing to concede just this one point to him. "It was perhaps the tiniest bit odd, though. And I did find myself puzzling over it just a bit. The conversation we ended up having wasn't the one I had imagined in my head for the last few months."

His eyes widened. "You've been imagining our conversations for months?"

Hannah sighed. "Okay, well, it's my turn to very much embarrass myself with words this time. But yeah, I have. I noticed you sitting there reading your book, wearing your slutty little glasses, which is what I believe the kids are calling them these days. And yeah, I've wondered what sort of conversation we might have." She pursed her lips. "I'm sure you haven't. And you probably think that our meeting at baggage claim was the first time we ever interacted."

"Well, that's true, though, isn't it?" he asked. "Sure, we've been seeing each other. I mean, not *seeing* each other, but, you know, seeing each other *around* for at least the last three months. But that was our first interaction. So I think it's safe to say that was our first meeting. Eye contact doesn't count, after all."

Hannah raised her eyebrows. "So you did recognize me?"

"Of course," he said. "I don't have face blindness, thankfully. It would make everything much harder if I did. But well...you and I have been taking a lot of flights together this these last weeks and months. It's become a nice sort of comfort looking up and seeing you there." He patted the armrest between them. "You sure do like sitting in this spot, don't you?"

Hannah nodded. "Clearly." She dipped her head towards the seats across from them. "And you like sitting there. I must say, it does surprise me. Sitting with your back to the counter? How will you know when they're about to start boarding?"

He pointed up towards the ceiling, where a voice was currently sounding through the loudspeakers. "Announcements are good for that," he said. "Plus, I can pretty well read your face to know what's happening. If, for example, the board changes to show that it's delayed, I'll see it in your demeanor before I hear it sung out from on high."

He gave her a devastating smile then. "So, thank you for that. You've spared me from having to turn around and crane my neck many a time."

Hannah felt hot and deliciously uncomfortable at the revelation that Handsome Guy had been paying such close attention to her. He had hidden it well, but now that he was admitting it, she couldn't help but feel self-conscious.

"Did I say something wrong?" He frowned at her. "Your face got all red just then. Almost like the sort of shade you'd see on an angry face in a cartoon. Did I upset you?"

She shook her head. "It isn't anger." When she saw no change in his puzzled expression, she sighed. He wasn't going to drop this, so before he started asking her if she was experiencing hot flashes, she might as well just tell him what was happening.

"It's something like shame," she said. "I believe I wasn't aware I had been so closely observed, and now that I *am* aware of it, some annoying part of my brain is racking my memories for all the different cringeworthy things you may have seen me do over these last months. I thought it was only *me* who was aware of *you*."

"Ah." He nodded. "You thought you were the only observer." He smirked at her then. "Interesting, that. You have no problem with surreptitiously observing me, even going so far as to write fan fiction about my glasses, by the sound of it. And yet the thought that I might also be observing you is taking things too far?"

She nodded. "Something like that. I know it doesn't make sense."

His smile was warm and broad. "I missed you two Sundays ago when I flew back to New York. I'm glad to see you today."

Hannah started at the abrupt change of topic, coupled with his vulnerable confession.

"You flew back that same weekend? You mean…just two days after we flew to London and your luggage gave me a piggyback ride? *That* Sunday?"

"That's the one. Technically, just one day after we arrived, since we landed Saturday morning."

"But…but why? Why would you fly in on Saturday morning and out on Sunday night? Do you hate yourself? Are you allergic to sleep?"

He gave her a close-lipped smile, but before he could begin to speak she gasped in recognition.

"It's because you fly business class, isn't it? Not being able to sleep is a totally foreign concept to you. I bet you arrive on either side feeling like you just walked out of a full-service salon. I bet the best meals and best sleeps of your life happen on these journeys. You probably schedule back-to-back flights just so you don't have to sleep in what's clearly a less comfortable bed in your Manhattan loft or London penthouse."

Handsome Guy sniffed. "You might be embellishing it slightly, but I do sleep pretty well. I'd say it's worth it for the upgrade for that alone." He narrowed his eyes at her. "I assume you're traveling for work…is your company not willing to spring for an upgrade?"

She barked out a laugh. "You know, I don't know. Can't say I've ever asked."

"No? Well, why not? The worst they can say is no."

"Is it really, though? I'm pretty sure the worst thing they can do is say no, then make a note of it in my file, bring it up at my annual performance review, and then fire me for not aspiring to the values of our company's core mission. I appreciate the suggestion, though."

"That's fair enough," he said. "I wasn't flying just to eat chef-quality airline meals, though."

"No? I'm shocked."

"Actually, no. I had a friend in a bit of a dire straits kind of situation, so I came back to give him a bit of a pep talk."

Hannah's jaw dropped. "You flew across an ocean just to be a good friend?"

He shrugged. "You say it like I flapped my very own arms to get there. The reality is that I'm flying back to London most weekends simply because I miss it and I have a life there, even if I do have this contract keeping me in New York for work."

"So essentially, you live in London and work in New York?"

"I..." He wavered. "Essentially, yes. It's not a daily commute I'm making, but I suppose it still counts even if I'm only doing it once a week. How about you? Traveling to London so regularly just for work? Do you have family there? A long-distance relationship?"

She chuckled at that. "For how often you see me at the airport, that would be a pretty one-sided relationship." She tilted her head to the side. "Though I guess if I was dating someone, you'd never see him since you'd be traveling in opposite directions. Passing like ships in the night. Not that you would recognize him, either."

"All perfectly valid points. So I guess it isn't the boyfriend thing. Just work then?"

Hannah nodded. "Splitting my time between two offices. I love it, though. That's why, when I have to go to London, I always take the Friday night flight. Trying to give myself as much extra time as possible to enjoy the city."

"So you're saying you prefer London to New York?"

She elbowed him in the arm. "Spoken like a true Londoner. No, I can love London and New York at the same time. I spend plenty of weekends in both cities, and they both have great things to offer."

"I haven't asked what you do, but based on that response, I'm going to guess you're some sort of diplomat."

"Not even close. I work in publishing."

They continued to chat, slipping into a companionable silence when the gate agents approached the counter and announced they would begin boarding soon. It was a clear enough signal that their time together was about to end, though for the briefest of flashes, Hannah let herself indulge in a wild hope. What if Handsome Guy had been so enamored by her and by the back-and-forth repartee they had enjoyed in the last half hour that he would switch his ticket and come see how the other half lives back in coach with her?

She twitched ever so slightly then, something like she was shaking her head but only for her own consumption. *Don't be ridiculous*, she told herself. *You might be great, but you're not "downgrading my luxury business class plane ticket to spend time with you" great.*

She got to her feet then, holding out her hand to Handsome Guy. "It was great chatting with you," she said, jerking her head towards the counter. "They're probably going to start boarding for you guys soon, so I'm just going to stretch my legs a bit. Take one last trip to the bathroom." She gave him a weak smile. "Maybe I'll see you on the other side."

He took her hand and shook it, his grip warm and strong. "I hope so."

Four

Over the course of a fairly standard flight, Hannah found her thoughts returning to Handsome Guy often. Why hadn't she thought to get his name, at least? Even more than that, why hadn't they exchanged numbers? It would have been easy enough to suggest, maybe under the pretext that they could split a cab to the airport in the future?

No, even that was ridiculous. You didn't just go around giving your phone number to a strange man, no matter how many times you had seen him reading a book and no matter how appealing his accent was. There was a proper way to do things, at least when it came to moving things from a crush to something more. Even if the "something more" was only ever going to be airport acquaintances, it still wasn't done to just immediately ask for someone's phone number and forsake the normal order of things.

As soon as the plane touched down, Hannah sent a message to Lane. Seven hours before, she had been so preoccupied by her interaction with Handsome Guy that she hadn't even bothered to send her regular "just about to take off!" message.

"Just landed! Don't suppose you're free to meet up?"

When Lane's response came through, it was a series of sad emojis. "Nooo! Totally forgot this was your next weekend in. I'm booked solid all day, but let's try to squeeze in a visit tomorrow? Xx"

Hannah sighed. If she'd ever wanted confirmation that her regular "just about to take off" messages were, in fact, serving a purpose other than annoying their recipients, then she had it.

"No worries!" she wrote back. "Have fun out there, and don't stress about tomorrow. I'm sure we'll run into each other around the office!"

It was the thinnest of comforts, though, and they both knew it. The weeks that Hannah spent in Muldoon Publishing's London office were full of meetings that stretched to fill almost all of her time. It wasn't that she needed Lane to entertain her—by this time, she knew plenty of spots around the city she could enjoy on her own. But after their last visit, after all the sadness Lane was clearly experiencing about Stuart, it would have been nice to check in with her and reassure herself that her friend was recovering.

Clearly she's recovering, she told herself. *She didn't say she was staying at home and crying about him, did she? She's going out and having fun and living her life...maybe she's even met someone new.* Lane hardly needed Hannah to ground her back down to reality if she was really out there having fun.

The hits only kept coming when the plane arrived at the gate. Hannah had wondered if she would see Handsome Guy as they were deplaning—*what had you expected*, she chided herself, *that he would wait in the jetway for you, so eager was he to pick up their previous conversation?*—but to no avail. She caught a glimpse of him at passport control, but he was too far away for her to call his name, if she had even known it.

Then, of course, there was the fact that they had sorted themselves into different lines at passport control, with Handsome Guy flying through the one for UK citizens, while Hannah waited in a long line with her fellow Americans.

She had been comforting herself with the idea that they might do the most hilarious thing yet and reunite at baggage claim, but she heard herself say "Shoot" out loud when she remembered that she hadn't actually checked a bag this time around. The previous luggage kerfuffle had all been thanks to the training binders she was transporting, and until this moment she had been grateful not to be repeating that experience.

But now, she had no reason to go to the baggage claim area, and even her desire to see Handsome Guy again wasn't strong enough for her to embrace that odd behavior choice. There might be a person somewhere in the world whose hobby was waiting around for things, and that person might enjoy waiting at baggage claim for a suitcase that would never come...but Hannah wasn't that person. Plus, the only logical conclusion of how it would all end if she *did* go stand by the carousel in hopes of talking to her crush again was that he *would* come talk to her and wait with her and when the last piece of luggage had been picked up and the conveyor belt had stopped moving, he would know the truth. There had never been a bag with her name on it in the checked baggage.

And how embarrassing would it be to be caught being that desperate?

No, it wouldn't do. She had to leave the airport, and she had to make her way to her hotel. There was simply no other option. If she and Handsome Guy were meant to cross paths again, then it would be entirely up to serendipity to make that happen.

The rest of Hannah's weekend flew by, a blur of walks in green parks, takeaway meals from her favorite spots near the hotel, and a lot of Netflix time on her laptop in her room. She wasn't exactly feeling sorry for herself, but she didn't reach out to Lane again to see if she had some free time open up on Sunday. As much as Hannah would have enjoyed time with a friend, there was a difference between being the breezy, cool sort of friend that people actually wanted to spend time with and being needy and repulsive.

She had a philosophy of trying to stay so far away from the needy and repulsive end of the spectrum that she probably came across as aloof sometimes. Not that she cared, though. It was so much better than the alternative that she didn't even mind if she was misunderstood like that.

Besides, if Lane had been free, she would have let her know. She wouldn't forget about Hannah, would she?

By the time Monday morning rolled around, Hannah was thrilled to get to work. The casual greetings and smiles shared in the Muldoon Publishing office scratched the itch of social interaction that she had been leaving untouched since Friday afternoon.

"Hannah! There you are!" She felt more than heard Lane's words, since they came along with a rib-crushing hug. "I missed you this weekend."

Hannah felt a twinge at her friend's words. If she had missed her so much, then why hadn't she made a point of seeing her? "I missed you too," she admitted, opting then to forge on ahead as if everything was fine rather than putting herself or her friend in an uncomfortable position. "I was glad to hear you were getting out, though." She gave Lane a genuine smile. "I'm hoping that means you've made some good progress on the Stuart front, though." She raised an eyebrow. "Were you out with anyone fun?"

Lane visibly blanched as she recoiled. "Hell, no. I got roped into showing some of my dad's prospective clients a good time around the city." She shuddered. "By which I mean, my dad seemed to hope that by having his young, hip daughter—his words, not mine—with him, that it would be that much easier to close the deal? Who's to say, really? He suggested I bring Stuart along, but of course I just told him he was busy and did it myself."

Hannah blinked. "You...haven't told your parents that you broke up?"

Lane shook her head. "I haven't, and don't you dare judge me. You wouldn't have told them either if they were your parents."

"You're probably right about that." Hannah had met Lane's parents just once, and the fifteen minutes they had spent together at a picnic Muldoon Publishing had hosted had been stressful, to say the least. Kiara and Russel, Lane's parents, were a high-powered couple, a gallery owner and a network executive. They were the sort who seemed more likely to be spotted attending a royal wedding than sitting on a picnic blanket shooing away flies.

"Still, you will tell them at some point, won't you?" Hannah asked, her eyes scanning Lane's face for some deeper truth of how she was feeling, at the same time that she felt her phone buzzing in her hand with incoming notifications. She was going to need to leave for a meeting soon, and if she didn't get some reassurance that Lane was doing better, she was going to be only half in that meeting room while the rest of her worried about Lane's trajectory for recovering from this breakup.

"They'll know when they need to. *If* they need to. I mean, I suppose if I meet someone else, I'll need to do some explaining." Lane's lip lifted humorlessly at the corner. "But let's face it. It's not as if they're exactly waiting on the edge of their seats for news from my personal life. I'm surprised Dad even got Stuart's name right."

Hannah sighed as she gave Lane's upper arm a gentle squeeze. "We'll talk later," she said, pulling out her phone to double check the time. "I've got a meeting now, but maybe after work this evening?"

Lane winced. "Unlikely. I've been roped into even more boozing and schmoozing with my dad, if you can believe it." She shook her head. "I really don't know why I didn't say no to him. It's almost as if the thought that I could didn't even occur to me. Maybe I'm just actually so bored without Stuart around that I'll say yes to anything I'm asked. Better to be out with my dad's stodgy old clients than at home alone crying into an American-sized ice cream tub."

Hannah gave her friend an apologetic frown. "I'm sorry, bud. I wish I'd asked you first so you would have had to say yes to me instead. American-sized ice cream tubs are practically my specialty. Keep another evening free for me this week, okay?"

And then, before Lane could get another word in, Hannah was off, just managing to squeeze inside the conference room door before the stand-up meeting started.

·❤·❤·❤·❤·❤·

It wasn't until Hannah's last night in London that she and Lane managed to find some time to spend together. After the workday ended, the two of them made their way to a nearby pub, both well aware that if they had planned instead to head home and meet up later, there was a good enough chance that one or both of them wouldn't make it.

It had been an exhausting but productive week in the Muldoon Publishing London offices, and Hannah was leaving with a real sense of satisfaction with the progress they had made on acquiring US and UK translation rights for a new batch of French titles. Now that the teams in New York and London were both on equal ground, she wondered if the time would come where she would no longer need to have a foot in both worlds.

There was a pang of sadness at that thought. As much as she had resisted the frequent travel at the beginning, she had really come to love the way her schedule kept her on her toes and the fact that she hadn't actually had to choose between her two favorite cities.

Though now that she thought of it, if she *did* have to choose, she couldn't confidently say that she'd stay put in New York. The soft spot that London had in her heart seemed to be growing bigger by the day.

But she wasn't going to bother Lane with all of that tonight. No, the two of them had a long overdue conversation about Lane's heart at the top of their agenda, and Hannah was even forgoing the opportunity to catch her friend up on the developments with Handsome Guy in favor of giving her the support she so clearly needed.

"So," Hannah began when they were both seated at the bar with two pints headed their way. "Catch me up. Have you talked to Stuart? Any progress on that front?"

Lane sighed deeply. "Not even a little," she said. "Not a word."

Hannah recoiled. That didn't align with what she had known about Lane's ex-boyfriend. He had been so devoted, so committed. It was hard to believe that now he wasn't even speaking to her.

"But why?" she asked. "Surely, he misses you, and you miss him, and there are things the two of you need to talk about, right?"

"Well, he made it pretty clear that he didn't want to pressure me into doing anything I didn't want to do," said Lane. "And apparently he includes having a simple conversation with him on that list." She took a sip of her drink. "I can't make him do something if he doesn't want to, after all."

Hannah shook her head. "No, this isn't right. The two of you need to talk. I think he's giving you space, yes. But I also think...well, it sounds like he's afraid of pressuring you into something you don't want to do—"

"Right," interjected Lane. "That's literally exactly what he said."

"But I don't think you've had a chance to make it clear what you *do* want to do, or even what you're willing to do," continued Hannah. "Look, while you're feeling rejected because he's not talking to you, he's probably feeling rejected because you not talking to him confirms all his worst fears about it being over between the two of you. About you not wanting to follow him to Cornwall." She paused, letting her words hang in the air as she considered her next move.

"I don't know," she said finally. "I think you just have to consider this from both of your perspectives."

Lane shook her head. "That sounds exhausting. And I doubt anyone is encouraging *him* to consider it from *my* perspective. Sounds like the kind of expectation we have only of women in relationships, while we're quick to let men off the hook."

Hannah shook her head. "This isn't like that. I'm not talking about doing emotional labor for someone who's unwilling to do it himself. I'm talking about Stuart. He's a sensitive guy. He's a good man. And he's not oblivious. He's not oblivious at *all*. That's why I feel so sure that the silence between you is hurting him, too."

"Maybe..." Lane shrugged. "There's a chance, I suppose, that you're right. But I don't know. I think I feel more comfortable just accepting things the way they are instead of reaching out to him. That sort of feels like there's something a bit off about it, you know? It feels a bit desperate."

Hannah shook her head. "It's not desperate to prioritize communication. To get some clarity before letting something so precious just slip away. Just try it, okay?"

"I will. But not tonight." Lane picked up her drink. "What we are *not* going to do is drink too much and call our exes."

Hannah picked up her drink to meet her friend's in the air. "Cheers to that. I totally agree."

<h1 style="text-align:center">Five</h1>

On Hannah's flight back to New York, there was no sign of Handsome Guy at the airport, and once again she felt disappointment on a level that did not match how well she actually knew this man. There was no reason for her to feel let down that a stranger, a man whose name she still didn't even know, wasn't going to be sitting far out of her eyeline up in business class on a flight that they were sharing over the Atlantic Ocean.

But since the two of them had started talking, had bridged the gap from merely noticing each other to actually interacting with each other, he had become a fixture on these journeys.

It was similar enough to having a crush on someone back in middle school, and rounding every corner with that bubble of anticipation that he might be there, that she might get to see him. She had been an expert in that field as a teen and there had often been a particular route she needed to take between two classes, sealed by the fact that *once* she had seen her crush at a water fountain. And so every time she traversed the halls between band class and pre-calculus, she had to take that same scenic detour in hopes that it actually *would* be scenic.

I suppose that's an unexpected perk, she told herself. *Having a crush as a full-grown adult does make me feel young inside.* Still, there was something about the word "crush" that just about curdled her insides.

And that was why she could never use that word when talking about Handsome Guy with Lane, who was, to date, the only person who knew of his existence in her life.

Hannah's flight back to New York was uneventful and not restful at all. It felt longer than normal, though as she tracked the progress of the plane over the map on the screen in front of her, she could confirm that it was just the same as normal.

No, the pilot hadn't made an unexpected stop over Greenland or taken the long way around. It was just that the novelty of the journey had entirely worn off, and in its place there was nothing but the exhaustion of it. The slog of another sleepless night and the knowledge that it was going to wear on her, that she was going to feel out of sorts and jet-lagged for at least the next few days.

And, of course, that she had another flight back to London less than a week later. As she waited outside JFK for her ride home, she shook her head and chided herself. *Enough already. I have* got *to talk to the powers that be and see if there's any way to make this journey a little more tolerable.*

There was a thrill of excitement at what was about to happen, due at least in part to the fact that asking for what she wanted was such a foreign concept. She felt guilty thinking about wasting the company's funds by asking for an upgrade, concerned that she was being too spoiled, thinking that she deserved better than they did. And if she had been in any other state besides exhausted and freshly off the plane, she would have talked herself out of it.

But as she slipped into the back of the car, she pulled out her phone and sent an email to her manager.

Dear Mr. Muldoon,

I have just returned from London and will be in the office tomorrow after I get some rest. The frequency of the flights has been wearing on me a bit, and I'm not as fresh and sharp as I would like to be the first day or so that I'm in London and then again in New York. I would love to have a conversation to see if there's any possibility of upgrading my seat on the flight so that there's more of a chance of getting some rest. If you have some availability, maybe we can talk about it tomorrow.

Best regards,

Hannah

She pressed send on the email, doing only a cursory glance for typos, but forbidding herself from agonizing too much over the proper send off. *Best regards, warm regards, sincerely...see you tomorrow.* None of them were exactly right.

At least with "best regards," she had seemed to land on the side of being both pleasant and formal.

As she read over the email she had sent, she was pleased to see that her exhaustion seemed to have forced a directness out of her that was uncharacteristic. It sounded like the sort of email that her manager would write, one where he was making a request but not tempering it with lots of "just asking" and "no problem" or "no worries." He would simply let her know what he wanted or expected with no apology.

Normally, Hannah was more inclined to send emails that read something like, "if it's not too much trouble, could you please find a way to do this thing? It's just that I really need it as soon as you can do it, but if not, no problem at all!"

In her current state, Hannah had no patience to write that sort of message. At the same time, she felt a twinge of discomfort at the email she had actually written. It was direct, but was it too direct?

She switched off her phone and leaned her head back. She didn't have the energy or the ability to stay awake to think about this right now.

･❤ ･❤ ･ ❤ ･❤ ･❤ ･

The next morning, a very groggy Hannah shuffled around her apartment, getting ready to head into the office. She groaned as she opened the fridge in hopes of finding some milk to put in her coffee.

Of course there was no milk. Nobody had been here for the last week to do any shopping, so why would there be?

She felt worse that morning than she had in a long time, and she wondered, not for the first time, if all this travel was finally doing her in, or—and she shuddered at the thought—if she was actually getting too old to keep doing this. She didn't want to consider that possibility, of course, and it didn't feel quite right. After all, she was barely 30, and the business lounges at the airports were full of men her age and older.

"Well, of course, we know their secret," she grumbled, pulling out her phone to see if Mr. Muldoon had replied to her email.

She had fallen asleep so soundly yesterday, and then slept for...glancing at the time on her phone, she could confirm it had been 11 hours. Only now, as she was reentering the land of the living, could she even remember that she had sent that message on the way home.

There was a new email, a response to her message, and she tapped on it with some trepidation. She reached for her mug to take a sip of black coffee to strengthen her resolve.

The email was short, just one line. He had written, **"See Betty when you come in."**

Hannah recoiled slightly as the words landed, pulling a face. Mr. Muldoon wanted her to talk to his assistant. He didn't want to have this conversation himself, apparently, and he considered it something worth delegating. True,

Betty was a very capable assistant, but she didn't have the same authority that Mr. Muldoon did. Hannah couldn't help but worry that this was his way of brushing her off. Maybe Betty was going to explain the budget to her, or maybe Betty was going to give her a slap on the wrist for even daring to ask for something so inappropriate.

Hannah took another sip of her coffee, wincing at the bitterness. She was too tired and too disoriented to worry much about what this meeting with Betty had in store.

In an uncharacteristic moment of acceptance, she sighed. There was no changing what was about to happen, and she would deal with it to the best of her ability when it did.

Eleven hours of sleep plus a long hot shower had worked a bit of magic on Hannah's overall well-being, but by the time she had completed her 30-minute commute to the office, she was no longer feeling as bright-eyed and alert as she had after stepping out of her shower.

Once she made it to the offices and through the lobby security up to the floor where Muldoon Publishing was located, Hannah dropped all of her things on her desk and made a beeline to the kitchen to make a proper cup of coffee. She hadn't even switched on her computer yet, but this was a priority. It had to be.

On her way to the kitchen, she greeted her co-workers that she hadn't seen in a week, smiling and nodding at their familiar refrains of, "Oh, look who's back in the office," and, "How's the jet lag treating you, kiddo?" It was rare that she heard a unique greeting on these sorts of mornings. Instead, it was mostly just shuffling through a Rolodex of jokes about how her colleagues never knew when they were going to see her in the office and how she must not even know what time zone she was on and how it must be nice to live such a jet-set lifestyle.

She smiled and nodded and gave them the responses they wanted. It didn't feel like there was anything particularly jet-set about this level of jet lag, but she knew not to complain to them. The jokes they made often sounded like they came from a place of envy, like her junior colleagues thought her level of travel was just the coolest thing ever. And some of her senior colleagues, who may have previously had the chance to do this sort of travel, were now focused only on the travel aspect of her role and not on the work side of things.

But it wasn't all meals with views of the Thames or Big Ben, or searching to find the pub with the best fish and chips.

No, Hannah wasn't playing tourist in London. She was working there. *And* she was working in New York. And even though it was one job split between the two countries, sometimes it felt like it was two full-time jobs, five hours apart in time zone, and that it was all becoming more than one person could handle.

"There you are," came Betty's voice from the doorway of the kitchen. "Welcome back, honey. How are you feeling?"

Hannah turned to face the older woman with a smile. She had always liked Betty. "I'm all right," she said. "Glad to be back. It's nice to see you."

Betty's face crumpled with concern. "Oh, honey. Not to be unkind, but you look exhausted, you poor thing. Did you sleep at all on the plane?"

Hannah shook her head and took a sip of the coffee, smiling at this cup of the perfect brew. "I never do," she said, "but it's okay. I slept for a good long time when I got home."

Betty shook her head. "Well, that won't do. No, it might be all right to stay up all night here and there when you're 21, or when it's occasional travel, like a honeymoon or something. But when you are traveling as often as you are—" She stepped closer and lowered the volume of her voice. "Well, it's high priority that you are more comfortable and able to rest better. Otherwise, you'll be no good to our colleagues in London and probably no good to us here, either." She winked at Hannah, then nodded at her cup of coffee. "Bring that with you to my desk, okay? I've got something to talk to you about."

Hannah was too intrigued to even think twice. She just nodded and said, "I'm following you there right now."

Whatever anticipation she had felt about this meeting, whatever concern she had had that Mr. Muldoon might be trying to talk her out of something, or that she might have overstepped with her request, all of that was gone now. Betty had the air of a kind aunt who was just looking out for her niece, just trying to make sure that she squeezed every last drop out of the perks of the job she had. And Hannah was all too ready to learn from her.

Betty slid in behind her computer, gesturing to a nearby chair so that Hannah could pull it over and sit right next to her. Even from that gesture alone, it was clear that working through this with Betty was the right choice. Mr. Muldoon was by and large an understanding boss, but he was more of the old school of thinking, keeping his cards close to his chest and making sure the chairs in his office—which were *never* brought around to sit next to his—had lower seats than his, so he could use that towering position to intimidate.

Betty, in contrast, was typing away at the screen, opening up a page Hannah had never seen before, but that had her name at the top, and a large number next to it. "What is this?" Hannah asked, pointing to her name and to the number. She couldn't even register at first how many digits were in the number, but as her brain came online, she saw there were seven.

"This is your miles account," said Betty. "Your company credit card, the same one we use to book all your flights, is a miles credit card. And between that and the flights themselves, you've been accruing miles even before you started these regular trips to London."

Hannah's eyes widened. "I never paid any attention to frequent flyer programs," she said. "I figured they were some kind of scam, that you'd have to travel way too much for them to even reap any benefits."

Betty shook her head. "A lot of people think that, but it's not always true. Plus, honey, you *do* travel a lot. If someone had to travel more than you in order for it to make sense to collect miles, well then, I guess they'd have to be a pilot or a flight attendant."

"That's true. A valid point." She smiled at Betty. "So why are you showing me this? What can I do with them?"

"Well, honey, I'm going to give you control of this account. First of all, you should have already that, since it's in your name. But the really cool thing is you can use these miles to upgrade your flights to get yourself bumped up into business class."

"Oh," said Hannah. "How many miles does that take? Would it use them all up?" If she was only going to be flying business class once, it would be good to know, so she could make sure to enjoy it but not get used to is.

Betty shook her head and chuckled. "Oh, no, you don't need a million miles for one upgrade. It's a lot less than that. Plus, they run some deals sometimes, so you'll be good for a long time just using these miles. And even if they run out—" She lowered her voice again. "I'm the one booking the flights, and I'll make sure you're sitting in business class in a comfy chair where you are able to get some sleep to arrive in London or back here feeling fresh as a daisy. Sound good?"

Hannah nodded and whispered back. "Yeah, it sounds really good. Thank you."

"Don't mention it, honey. This should have been taken care of ages ago. I don't know how Mr. Muldoon managed to overlook it, and I can't believe you didn't say something sooner. From here on out, though, you're traveling in style." Her fingers were flying over the keyboard as she talked, and Hannah felt a weight lift from her chest.

Six

Hannah arrived at the airport earlier than ever on the following Friday afternoon, heading there straight from the office. After Betty had showed her how to navigate the airline miles website and had booked her next flight with a built-in upgrade, Hannah had felt a tingle of possibility. Worrying her lower lip, she had asked the older woman if there was any chance she would be able to upgrade this week's flight since it was already in the system.

"Of course, sweetheart," Betty had replied. "Just give me your confirmation number and we can get that sorted right now."

As Hannah had repeated the series of random numbers and letters, she had let herself wonder for the first time if this was finally going to be her opportunity to sit next to Handsome Guy on a flight.

Don't be greedy, she told herself. *As if flying in business class isn't enough, now you need to choose your seat partner, too? If it's meant to be, he'll be there. And if he isn't, maybe you can just move on from this whole "crush" thing.*

She had forced herself to put Handsome Guy out of her mind for the rest of the week, but now, as she walked through the doors of the airport, she found herself wondering again what the odds were that he would be on this flight—and if he were, would they be sitting in each other's chattable zone? What kind of cruel twist of fate would it be to finally be in the same cabin as Handsome Guy and not even be near enough to each other to exchange a glance or two and a casual word of greeting?

When she checked in for her flight, the check-in officer smiled. "You could have used that counter over there," she said, gesturing to her right. "It's a much shorter line."

"I...sorry, what?" Hannah asked, looking in the direction the woman was pointing.

"It's the business class check-in line," she replied, her eyes kind. "Make sure you remember that for next time, so you don't end up waiting in this long line."

"Oh, I don't mind waiting." Hannah leaned forward, dropping her voice. "Sorry, it's my first time flying business class and clearly I don't know what I'm doing." She could feel her cheeks growing warm. "If there was ever a sign that I didn't belong here, I'd say this is it."

The agent shook her head. "Not at all. It just takes a little getting used to. You belong there as much as anyone else does." It was her turn to lean closer, her tone almost conspiratorial. "Just don't forget that your international business class ticket grants you access to our lounge, okay? I just couldn't live with myself if I thought you were sitting at the gate eating an overpriced sandwich when there's all that free food and relative comfort waiting for you there."

"Oh...right!" Hannah forced her lips upwards, hoping she could convince at least one of them that she had been aware of the lounge access. Betty hadn't mentioned it to her, but then she *had* probably assumed that Hannah knew her way around the airport by now.

And what was it she had said about how this all should have been sorted out a lot sooner? Did that mean that Hannah was the only one to blame for not speaking up about her wishes?

She took her carry-on bag and made her way towards security, noticing once again that there was a separate line for business class passengers. It felt oddly uncomfortable to step into it, like she was putting herself somewhere she didn't belong and everyone else knew it too.

She forced herself to hold her chin high, trying to recall some old lesson about how faking confidence could actually force you to feel some semblance of it. It wasn't working yet, but maybe these kinds of things just took time.

As she snaked her way through the line, she thought again about Betty and about the whole upgrade debacle only coming to pass because her sleep-deprived alter ego had dared to send an email without her usual number of filters. When she stripped away the ways she toned herself down for mass consumption, it seemed there was a normal human woman underneath, someone with dislikes and desires and even the ability to express both of those things.

Maybe there was something to this whole idea of speaking up for herself, of expressing what she wanted.

The TSA agent greeted her with a smile and she flew through the business class security screening, though that now familiar feeling that she was an imposter, that she didn't belong here, that everyone could tell she didn't know what she was doing, came back with a vengeance.

This is getting ridiculous, she told herself. *If I can't let myself enjoy the luxuries of business class, then what even is the point of any of this?* Hannah resigned herself to continuing to push herself out of her comfort zone, making her way to the lounge, even though the sight of it stirred up more discomfort, more of that imposter syndrome.

She was greeted at the door by a smiling man who scanned her boarding pass and welcomed her by name a second later. Inside the lounge, inside this space she had only ever let herself dream about, she found seating that was far more comfortable than anything she'd ever seen at the gate, and a veritable smorgasbord of food and beverage that she knew was all complimentary. She wouldn't reveal herself as the imposter that she knew she was by asking how much the various items cost.

She put on a smile, trying to remember to put her shoulders back and her chin up, to have the confidence of someone who did this all the time, and then she claimed a seat with a great view of the runway. She sank into the luxurious leather and audibly sighed at how comfortable it was. "I could get used to this," she murmured, aware that that was precisely the danger. If she did get used to it, would she ever be able to go back to her old ways?

She heard the sound of a throat clearing and looked to her left to find a young woman sitting there smiling at her kindly. "Sorry," the woman said, "but is it your first time flying business class too?"

Hannah chuckled. "Is it that obvious?"

"No, no, of course not," the woman rushed to explain. "I just meant…well, I heard you say something like, I could get used to this, and…yeah, that sounded like… Well, it sounded like me when I walked into the lounge half an hour ago."

"It's your first time, too?"

The woman nodded. "It is. It never made sense to me to waste my miles on an upgrade when I could use them for booking economy flights instead. But my fiancé insisted. He said I'm always so exhausted after those economy flights and that it might be nice for me if I could enjoy the travel itself a little more and maybe even get some rest."

Hannah nodded. "That is almost exactly what I'm doing too, except it's my job and not my fiancé that's asking me to get more comfortable with this level of luxury." She darted a glance toward the tables of food. "I'm not sure I can ever get used to it, though."

The woman smiled. "Why don't we go check out the food together?" she asked. "There's nothing to be afraid of. Nothing that we need to do to qualify us to belong there. If you're hungry or thirsty, that's enough."

"Okay then." Hannah got to her feet beside the woman. "Let's do it."

It was more comfortable to explore her options with someone beside her and with Sandra, the young woman, she could almost make herself believe that she fit in here. When they returned to their chairs with plates piled with a sampling of everything on offer and a tall glass of champagne each, at first they began to eat in silence.

Before long, though, Hannah couldn't stop herself from speaking what was on her mind.

"Do you feel like you don't belong here?" she asked. "Not that I think you don't. I just mean…well, I feel that way. I'm having a really hard time with every step of this process. I'm not sure if I'll be able to keep this up or if I'll just end up insisting that my company fly me coach and use my miles for something else."

Sandra shook her head. "It's so normal to feel like you don't belong when you're in a new place. I mean, it would be borderline sociopathic if you *did* walk into a completely new experience with a much more luxurious way of life than anything you know and you were just like, 'Yep, I belong here. This is my place.'" She shook her head. "That would be bizarre, actually."

Sandra looked around, nodding towards the men and women sitting near them. "I bet they all felt that the first time, too. It's just that now they've been doing it so long that they're completely accustomed to it." She shook her head. "So don't let your brain tell you that you don't belong here. Just persist. Get through today. Get through your return flight and remind yourself as often as you need to that you *do* belong here. That it's safe for you to be here. That it's okay for you to experience this comfort and…yeah." She held up her glass and nodded towards her plate. "Just enjoy the small things rather than thinking about class and comfort and the whole concept of deserving something. Just think about how tasty these food items are and how nice the champagne bubbles feel. Take it one bubble at a time. That way, you'll get all the way to your destination and by the time you get there, you won't feel like this anymore."

Hannah was quiet as she considered her new friend's words. "I can't promise to get that right on my first try," she said finally, "but I *can* promise to keep trying. How about you?"

"Oh, totally." Sandra's smile was sheepish. "I'm saying this all to you like I've got it figured out already, but just know that those were all words I needed to hear, too."

"Then I'm in good company." Hannah raised her champagne flute to toast her friend. "Who knows, maybe we'll run into each other in another lounge like this someday."

"I'll keep an eye out for you," said Sandra as their glasses clinked against each other.

As they slipped into a companionable silence, Hannah couldn't help but think about the first person she'd had this sort of airport-based relationship with. The first person she actually had run into often enough at the airport to really notice him, to have one part of her awareness always scanning the perimeter for him. Not that it had taken multiple exposures to notice Handsome Guy. She had been aware of him from the first time he had taken a seat across from her, and it would take months with no exposure to him before she stopped looking for him around every corner, if that time ever came.

Glancing around the lounge, she wasn't surprised not to see him, though that didn't stop a pang of disappointment from making itself known in her belly. It seemed unlikely that Handsome Guy spent much time in airport lounges, judging by the fact that he was always right where she could see him, waiting at the gate.

That thought triggered a flutter of excitement. Was he doing the same thing she was, hanging around the gate in hopes of catching a glimpse of her?

She pulled a book from her carry-on and resolved to lose herself in the pages. If Handsome Guy was on her flight, she wouldn't know it until they were boarding. There was nothing she could do now to get that information, not unless she wanted to leave the comfort of the lounge to go off in search of him. She took a nibble of her bagel and shook her head. She was going to enjoy this experience while she had it and convincing herself that she belonged here was her task for the next couple of hours. Finding out if she was seated next to Handsome Guy on the plane was a task for Future Hannah to worry about.

❤ • ❤ • ❤ • ❤ • ❤

Hannah and Sandra parted ways with a hug and a quick exchange of phone numbers. "For accountability," Sandra had said. "Because I'm going to check up on you and make sure you're letting your company pay for business class upgrades, and I hope you'll do the same for me."

"Of course," Hannah had replied. "I hope you enjoy your flight and every single bit of luxury that comes your way. And have fun in Amsterdam!"

"You, too," Sandra had replied. "Enjoy London, I mean. I know it's a work trip, but still."

Oh, I intend to enjoy it, thought Hannah, standing a little taller as she approached her gate, trying to peek over the passengers who were already standing in line, though boarding hadn't started yet. *And I'll enjoy it even more if I can just find...*

But she deflated then, her eyes passing over the last row of waiting passengers. There was no sign of him. Handsome Guy was nowhere to be found. Today, as it turned out, was *not* her lucky day.

As the gate agent called for the business class passengers to begin boarding, Hannah pulled her lips into her mouth and chuckled silently to herself. *Okay, let's not be dramatic,* she chided herself. *It definitely* is *my lucky day.*

Flying in business class was like a completely different experience than every other flight she had taken between New York and London. Not only was the food and drink—and the fact of its abundance—significantly better than anything she had previously eaten on an airplane, but being able to fully recline and put up her feet was definitely the best feature.

After eating a meal—a four course meal with real utensils, no less—she didn't even bother to peruse the entertainment system. She simply reclined, getting assistance from one of the flight attendants to turn her seat into its bed form.

Even with all the anticipation she had felt, all there was to experience and explore, it was still too comfortable for her to be able to stay awake and take it all in.

And so that was how Hannah spent her first experience in business class almost entirely unconscious.

♥ • ♥ • ♥ • ♥ • ♥

When the announcement came that they would be beginning their descent to London, Hannah woke up, stretched, yawned, and came back up to a seated position. "Oh my gosh," she said, looking out the window, "I feel great." And at the view of London approaching, she smiled, easily able to imagine herself out in those streets.

For once, it didn't feel like she needed to head straight to her hotel to take a nap or search out the nearest cafe to consume copious amounts of caffeine. This was an entirely different travel experience. In terms of how refreshed she felt at the end of her journey, it was like comparing sleeping on a bed of feathers while traveling to clinging to the side of the airplane with a death grip.

She thought back to her time in the lounge with Sandra and hoped her new friend was feeling the same now. There was no part of Hannah that felt like she didn't belong here, or like this wasn't a good use of resources. How could either of those things be true if she felt this good?

When the plane landed, Hannah took the time to send two quick messages. The first one was to Sandra sharing her verdict on the business class experience, and then the next one was to Lane, letting her know that she had arrived and would be up to spend some time together today. This time around she had remembered to text Lane in advance, so the previous day she had already gotten some assurance that Lane was not going to be spending this entire weekend showing her dad's clients around the city as some sort of personal tour guide.

Hannah completed her business class experience with effortless deplaning and getting to be in the early end of the passport control line. Once again, she had not packed a checked bag, and she was only too happy to roll her carry-on out the arrivals gate door. She smiled back at the airport as she left, making her way to the hotel shuttle, having the strange feeling that she was already looking forward to being back at Heathrow for her next flight.

She shook her head at herself. *Sure, it had been a good sleep on the plane and a comfortable bed to sleep in, but come on...you're in London now. Enjoy it.*

Seven

Several hours later, Hannah and Lane were talking on the phone. "I'm so sorry, love," Lane said. "I had meant to be all yours today, but then this last-minute thing came up and there was nothing I could do about it."

"Don't you worry about a thing," said Hannah. "I know my way around a last-minute thing. I understand. I promise I'm not secretly fuming at you over here. It's really okay."

She heard Lane sigh on the other end of the phone. "Well, now that it's all over, a few of us are thinking of going out tonight. Having a drink or two. But I guess you wouldn't—"

"No, I would actually," interjected Hannah. "I feel great, and I think it's time I took you up on one of these offers."

Lane was silent for a moment, her shock evident even without being able to see her face. "You...you...you're going to come out tonight?"

"That's what I'm trying to tell you, Lane," said Hannah. "This whole time it wasn't that I was a homebody or a hotel body, I guess it would be. It's just that I was so jet lagged and sleep deprived and didn't know what end was up. I hate to say it, but flying business class and actually being able to get some rest..." She's let out some air. "It's a game changer. I feel like a new woman."

"Okay then, New Woman. Looks like we're going to have some fun tonight. Do you want to meet us at the pub?"

"Yeah, that sounds great," said Hannah. "Just text me the location."

"Will do." The smile in Lane's voice was palpable. "I've got a surprise for you, and I think you're going to like it."

With those words, Lane ended the call, leaving Hannah to wonder what sort of adventure awaited her.

•♥•♥•♥•♥•♥•

When Hannah walked into the door of The Black Dog that evening, it took her eyes a moment to adjust to the low light inside. The sun hadn't yet set, but inside the pub was as dark as its namesake.

"Over here!" Lane's voice called from her left, a moment before Hannah felt herself pulled into a familiar embrace.

"You made it!" Lane cried, her mouth so close to Hannah's ear that she could feel her warm breath.

"Sure did, just like I said I would." Hannah grinned at her friend as their hug ended. "You look really happy," she noted. "What's...?"

But her question died on her lips as she took in two familiar men standing behind Lane, both looking at her with vastly different expressions on their faces.

Over Lane's left shoulder, she could see Stuart, and the smile he was wearing matched Lane's. But over Lane's right shoulder—and even more puzzling—was none other than Handsome Guy, and his gaze was locked on Hannah. Judging by the heat she could feel in her cheeks, his attention had been on her since the moment she had entered the bar.

"How...? What...? Why...?" Hannah shook her head, looking first between Lane and Stuart. "Are you two...?" Off their nods, she felt her shoulders release some of their tension. "Great. I definitely want to hear more about this." She locked her eyes on Handsome Guy then, speaking directly to him for the first time in weeks. "And you...?"

Lane piped up then. "Hannah, this is Stuart's friend, Guy. We wanted to introduce the two of you before..." She chuckled softly then. "Well, we wanted to introduce you before we made the colossal mistake of breaking up, but now that we're back together and you're actually out with us for a night on the town, there's no time like the present, is there? Anyway, Guy travels a lot, just like you, and Stuart said he had a great story about rescuing a damsel in distress at baggage claim that you might really enjoy."

"Are you...?" Hannah leaned closer to her friend. "Are you shitting me right now?"

"Not at all. I haven't heard the story myself, but that's just because Stuart and I are still reconnecting and we've had other things to talk about."

Hannah looked at Stuart then. "So then, are *you* shitting me?"

Stuart cleared his throat. "I can assure you I am not. Lane and I are indeed back together and we owe a lot of that to Guy here. He was the one to tell me to talk to her and ask her what she wanted rather than assuming I knew what it was." He gave her a soft smile. "Of course, it sounds like we owe you a debt of gratitude on that same front, too. If you hadn't encouraged my beautiful girlfriend to speak up to me, then the two of us might not be right here in front of you."

Hannah nodded, her gaze landing back on Guy then. "I am deeply glad that the two of you are back together, and I'm going to want to hear all about it before the night is done." She swallowed, addressing Guy for the first time then. "So, are *you* shitting me? Because it really seems like someone here is playing a practical joke on me." She looked around. "Is this some sort of rogue reality television spot? Hidden cameras behind the bar?"

Guy spoke up for the first time then, and his voice was even deeper, even better than she had remembered it being. "There's no practical joke happening, Hannah, and I'm just as surprised as you are to meet you again here."

"You two know each other?" Stuart asked, wrinkling his brow.

"We've met," said Guy, a small quirk of a smile playing at his lips. "At baggage claim, in fact."

"Is this—?" Stuart began, his eyes darting between Guy and Hannah. "Are you—?"

"Are you Handsome Guy?" Lane blurted, studying Guy's face and then Hannah's. "Is he Handsome Guy?"

Hannah nodded. "He is, though I didn't realize just how on the nose that nickname was."

"And you're the damsel in distress that he rescued."

Guy cleared his throat. "I never used that phrase, Stuart. That was your own interpretation. While I did rescue Hannah from the baggage carousel, I would never refer to her as a damsel in distress."

Gazes were darting about every which way, with Lane and Hannah exchanging looks and Stuart and Guy doing the same. Then, Stuart and Hannah. Stuart and Lane. Guy and Lane. But the last, most lingering one was between Guy and Hannah.

Lane nudged Hannah from behind. "It seems like the two of you have some talking to do." She grabbed Stuart's elbow, steering him away. "And of course we do, too. We'll just be over here if you need us."

And before Hannah could stop her friend, Stuart and Lane were gone, and she was alone with Guy. His presence was a tangible thing, even when she wasn't looking at him.

"I've wanted to ask this for a very long time," he began, and she could hear him smiling. "Can I buy you a drink?"

Hannah turned her head to look at him, finding a man in front of her who was partly familiar and partly an enigma. For as often as she had replayed her memories of their previous interactions, what she saw in front of her now didn't match.

He seemed bigger, somehow, and yet calmer, too. He had this presence that was somehow both hulking and comforting. There was something grounding about him, something about his broad chest that made her want to step a little closer and let his arms come wrap around her.

"I would really love that," she said.

When the two of them were settled in a nook a few moments later with their respective pints of cider and Guinness, Hannah worried for just a second that they wouldn't know what to talk about or that the conversation wouldn't match up to what it had been in her head. Maybe she was about to find out that despite how easy it had seemed to be around Guy, the contents of the tin didn't exactly match what was on the label, and talking to him he would actually prove to be insufferable.

But then he spoke.

"I've been flying economy," he said, "hoping to find you. But you've been nowhere to be found. I definitely didn't expect you to walk in here tonight."

"You've been flying economy for me?" She smiled at him. "Then you'll be thrilled to hear what I did today for the first time."

"Oh?" He raised an eyebrow. "If you've discovered some new hack for booking the cheapest flight by agreeing to sit in the bathroom whenever it's vacant or be stuffed into the overhead compartment, then please do tell. I'm all ears."

Her elbow found his, a playful joust of a gesture. "It's not that. I actually flew business class today for the first time."

His eyes had gone wide. "And what did you think?"

She took a sip of her cider. "I think I had no idea what I was missing out on this whole time. But why were you squeezing yourself into a seat in coach?" she asked. "And especially when you didn't even see me at the airport?"

Guy's hand came up to the back of his neck and something like discomfort passed across his face. "It might have been some misguided attempt at controlling fate," he said, wincing slightly. "After I didn't see you on one of my flights, I had a bit of a think and decided that perhaps I could control fate or destiny or whatever you want to call it simply by being willing to sacrifice what I held most dear."

Hannah nodded. "And naturally, what you hold most dear is lounging comfortably in the business class cabin."

He gestured towards his long legs. "These bad boys don't make it particularly comfortable," he admitted, "but still, I just had this feeling that if I made some kind of sacrifice, I would be rewarded by finding myself sitting right next to you and the two of us would have five uninterrupted hours to get to know each other."

He took a sip then. "It does seem as if it has worked, even if it didn't work in the most direct way."

"Is that so?" Her smile felt playful. "Are you being rewarded right now by having me here? Are all of your sacrifices paying off?"

He reached for her and his warm hand encircled hers. "I don't know if this is happening because of my sacrifice or not, but it absolutely feels like I'm being rewarded right now."

That was how it felt to Hannah, too.

The next morning, Hannah and Lane had plans to meet for breakfast and debrief. The message had landed on Hannah's phone in the middle of her second drink with Guy, at the moment just before Lane and Stuart were headed home for the evening.

Hannah and Guy had both been red-cheeked and a bit mumbly while saying goodbye to their friends, and if he had been feeling anything like what she had been feeling, then they were both probably a little embarrassed to be caught so obviously having a crush in front of their friends.

Lane had squeezed Hannah tightly, whispering in her ear for only her to hear. "It's going well, right? Should I take you with me, give you a reason to duck out?" But when Hannah had mumbled back that that wouldn't be necessary, Lane had only hissed again. "Tomorrow morning, missy. You're telling me everything."

And that was precisely how the two friends found themselves sitting on a bench beside the river, sipping coffee from to-go cups at eight o'clock in the morning. Hannah had said she was too wired to sit in a restaurant and use cutlery, so they had walked and talked until they'd found this perfect spot.

"So it was really everything you'd hoped it would be?" Lane asked, draining the rest of her cup. "Turning the fantasy into reality didn't disappoint? I shouldn't be alarmed at Stuart's terrible taste in friends? Though, to be honest, Guy *is* actually my friend, too, so that wouldn't reflect well on me either, would it?"

"He was great," said Hannah, trying to bite back a smile. "I can't even remember who I imagined him to be before we properly met. The real thing is just so...present. He's the best listener, has a great sense of humor, and I can't imagine ever getting sick of him."

"Hmm." Lane nodded in agreement. "He's a fab friend, too, which should definitely count for something. He talked sense into Stuart the same way you did for me, so it sort of sounds like the two of you are made for each other."

Hannah knew her cheeks had to be maroon at that comment, and she tried to play it off with a laugh. "Let's not march right down the wedding aisle." She gave her friend a tentative smile. "To start with, I think we'll just head down the airplane aisle." She winced. "Too cheesy?"

Lane's eyes were wide as she leaned forward. "Are the two of you coordinating your flights already? Because for two people who travel as much as you both do, that's practically the same as moving in together. It might mean you spending the same amount of time together as a couple who does actually lives in the same apartment, though we can compare statistics after Stuart and I do just that."

Hannah blinked. "You're moving to Cornwall?"

Lane nodded. "That's the plan. It turns out, all I wanted was to be near him and all he wanted was to make sure I got what I wanted, so that works out nicely. It's just temporary, you know. I'm not saying we're going to settle down on the Cornish coast and never return to London, but..." She shrugged. "I'm not *not* saying that either. You and Guy will have to come visit us when we get settled."

"I..." Hannah sighed. "I'm not good with this whole 'publicly displaying my affection' thing, but...I think I'd actually really like that. I have a good feeling about him. About us. About the fact that we bumped into each other over and over again, only for it to turn out that we have freaking mutual friends and I would have met him ages ago if I'd just spoken up for myself sooner and asked for the upgrade and actually been well rested enough to go out one of the many times you invited me."

"That's a lot of 'ands.'" Lane reached over to squeeze Hannah's hand. "But I think the more important thing here is that you spoke up for yourself and asked for what you wanted and things got immeasurably better once you did." She paused, rattling her empty cup and preparing to stand. "I guess the only question, then, is what do you want when it comes to Guy? And are you going to speak up to make sure you get it?"

Eight

The following Sunday, Hannah had butterflies in her stomach as she waited for Guy to pick her up to head to the airport. They had each been too busy to get together since their initial meeting, and she hadn't seen him since the previous Friday evening.

The texts had been abundant, though, so even if there was a part of her that wondered if the magic had been real, she could scroll back through a week of messages and reassure herself. She did just that while waiting for him to arrive.

On Saturday, he had written to her first.

"Good morning, Hannah. It's Guy, in case you didn't save my number yet. I had a great time with you last night and would love to see you again. The rest of this weekend is unfortunately fully booked with prior family commitments (Granddad's 95th), and I'm flying back to New York on Sunday. When is your flight?"

"Good morning, Guy. Of course I saved your number...it's saved as Handsome Guy, to no one's surprise. My flight is next Sunday. Are you coming back that soon, already?"

"If it means us getting to actually fly together, then absolutely. But actually, a friend of mine is getting married next weekend, so let that take some pressure off. I'm not flying over the ocean just to spend time with you, though that doesn't mean I wouldn't consider it..."

The messages had continued throughout the week, from a detailed recap of Guy's grandfather's birthday bash—"You would have loved it, but I did think it might be just a smidge too soon to meet the family"—all the way through his journey back to New York, complete with extreme gratitude at once again being back in business class.

For her part, Hannah had tried her best to keep the communication going too, holding tight to her recently learned lesson about expressing herself and speaking up for what she wanted. It felt like too much to put it into writing—and in a text message, of all things—just how much she liked Guy and just how curious she was about where this thing between them might be headed.

But still, as she scrolled through the last of their messages and checked the time, she felt that nervous flutter. She needed to speak up today, and she couldn't be sure she would ever actually get what she wanted if she didn't do that.

A car pulled over to the side and stopped just in front of her hotel, the passenger side window rolling down. She leaned forward to see Guy there, smiling up at her.

"Hello there!" he said, wincing as the words came out a little too loudly. He chanced a glance in his rearview mirror and frowned at the traffic there. "I would come around and open the door for you, but if I even open my door, someone's likely to take it off."

Hannah shook her head as she was opening the door, sliding in beside him and placing her carry-on down by her feet. "It's not a problem at all. And hello to you too!" She let out a nervous chuckle. "It's a little odd, isn't it?"

Guy flicked on his turn signal and maneuvered back into the flow of traffic, giving her a quick glance and a much longer nod. "It is, indeed. I wish I had seen you again much sooner than this, and the texting seemed like a decent substitute...until you're there in front of me again and I just lose all sense of cool."

A laugh escaped Hannah's lips at that. "I think it might be to our benefit that we can't keep up any sort of illusion of coolness."

"No game playing, you mean?"

She nodded. "Yeah, I guess that's the perk of the way we've gotten to know each other. You've seen me at my most embarrassing—"

"As have you," he cut in. "I still think of the odd way I behaved when we met at baggage claim, and it makes me wince every time."

Hannah reached a hand over and patted his hand where it rested on the gearshift. "Don't feel bad. You were charming, and if nothing else, that was a memorable meet-cute."

He darted a glance at her before returning his gaze to the traffic. "So that's what it was? A meet-cute? The beginning of an epic love story?"

Dang it. Did I mean to just blurt that out right here in the middle of Sunday rush hour?

"Well…" Hannah took a deep breath and went for it. "I think so. I hope so, I guess. If that's what you want too, of course," she hurried to add.

As the car came to a stop at the next traffic light, Guy reached for her, pulling her face towards his and dropping a quick kiss on her forehead. The electricity that zinged through her body at that contact felt like she had touched a live wire and she gasped slightly.

"It's definitely what I want," he said as he pulled back, the cars around them beginning to move again. "And I hope this flight today is just the first of many we take together."

Hannah smiled. "I'd like that." And because she couldn't stop herself from wondering about it (and therefore couldn't stop herself from thinking out loud about it), she continued. "Do you think it will be a problem, though, that we're from different countries and live on different continents? What happens when your work contract is done or my responsibilities change?"

With his eyes still on the road, Guy placed his hand on hers. "You might be getting just a bit ahead of yourself, my dear." He lifted her hand then, placing a kiss across the back of her knuckles. "But I can assure you that whatever life hands us, we can figure out. Plus, there are always flights."

"That's true. I've got a bit of a soft spot for the red eye flight between New York and London."

"You and me both, love. You and me both."

Author's Note

Thanks for coming along for the journey with Hannah and Guy. I hope you enjoyed these two as much as I did in the writing process.

The next book in this series is called *Unexpected Turbulence*, and it is (for now, at least) the last of all airport-inspired love stories. All of the books in this "Catching Flights & Feelings" novella series can be read as stand-alones, so if you missed *At Your Altitude*, make sure to check it out.

To stay updated on other works in progress or purchase books and bundles directly from me, please visit my website at kcmccormickciftci.com.

If you loved this book, please consider leaving a review, as that is one of the best ways to support indie authors like me. Reviews left on major retail sites (wherever you bought this book is a great start!), Goodreads, and Book-Bub will help other readers discover this book, too.

About the Author

KC McCormick Çiftçi is an English teacher turned romance writer. She spent the majority of her twenties living and working abroad, collecting the experiences that inform the stories she tells. She enjoys telling multicultural and international love stories through romantic comedy and women's fiction. She lives in Turkey with her husband and a herd of cats.

Prior to diving into the world of romance, KC published two self-help books for intercultural couples, *Loving Across Borders* and *The K-1 Visa Wedding Plan*. Both are available wherever books are sold.

For updates on upcoming releases, behind the scenes news, and all my favorite book recommendations, visit kcmccormickciftci.com (or just point your phone camera at the QR code below).

Books by KC McCormick Çiftçi

Austen in Turkey
Pride, Prejudice, & Turkish Delight
Sense, Sensibility, & the Mediterranean Sea

Home (Abroad) for the Holidays
Christmas on Inishmore
Christmas at Terminal One
Christmas by the Sea

Intoxicated by You
Intoxicated by You

Cats of Istanbul
The Vet Upstairs
From Strays to Soulmates
Whiskers and Wanderlust

Choose Your Own Adventure
We Were Inevitable

Intercultural Relationship Self Help

Loving Across Borders
The K-1 Visa Wedding Plan